"There's many a poem in this glorious tome
to amuse and afear and delight.
I read the whole book beginning to end
and end to beginning one night...

In reading Ken Priebe's *Gnomes of the Cheese Forest and Other Poems* I was utterly captivated, not only by the eponymous gnomes and other fearsome and forlorn creatures that spring to life in the pages, but also by the heart at the center of the poems. More than once I turned a page laughing, only to be stilled by a quiet gentleness in the next entry. These poems are a delight and a comfort. I can't wait to introduce my favorite kids (and grownups) to my new favorite poet."

Laure Hittle, Director of Clearwater Library

"You could give it for Christmas! For birthdays! For fun!
Read a copy with Gram when she's 101!
But I'll tell you the very best why, how, and when:
This book is for revisiting childhood again.

Ken Priebe has written and illustrated a book that works like a box of magic, a bag of candy, a window into a dimension as mad as *The Muppet Show*, and an escape into playfulness as rewarding for adults as for kids. Parents will recognize wisdom in these preposterous poems, while kids will find a kindred spirit. Until another volume appears, I'll just keep rereading this one."

Jeffrey Overstreet, author of *The Auralia Thread* series

"Hark! The voice in my head's done gargling,
and is now prepared to recite,
to sing loud the chorus,
Gnomes of the Cheese Forest's a fantastical, magic delight!

My entire family loves *Gnomes of the Cheese Forest and Other Poems*. It is a rare and marvelous collection, an invitation to fun and wonder. It is book woven with a spell for conjuring delighted smiles. I am glad to have been enchanted."

S. D. Smith, author of *The Green Ember* Series

Gnomes of the Cheese Forest
and Other Poems

Written & Illustrated
by
Ken Priebe

Illustration for *A Butterfly in the Right Corner* (Page 79)
by
Ariel Lynn Priebe

For Jay, Ariel & Xander

*Thank you for making me laugh
and being the hearts I come home to.*

Text and illustrations © Copyright 2018 Ken A. Priebe
All rights reserved.
No part of this book may be reproduced or transmitted in any form
or by any means whatsoever without express written permission from
the author, except in the case of brief quotations embodied in critical
articles and reviews.

No gnomes, whip-poor-wills, smackle-bats or other creatures were harmed in the making of
this book, except for a carrier pigeon named Simon who was dispatched to the Lost Island of Spider
Zombies to obtain a bottle of the invisible ink needed to write *The Invisible Poem* on page 69. Simon
sustained minor injuries to his left wing, but he has fully recovered and can still play the clarinet beautifully.

Deepest thanks to Anne & Jeffrey Overstreet, David Robinson, Clint Morris, Jagjit Vagha, Jeff Balcerski,
Joe Sutphin, Laure Hittle, Laura Thomas, Luke Flaming, S.D. Smith, and all who have given their steadfast
support and encouragement.

Cover and Title Font: Beyond Wonderland by Chris Hansen
Text Font: Adobe Garamond Pro

ISBN 978-1-7752559-0-1

Priebelieving Press
Delta, BC Canada

Table of Contents

Page
9 ~ Gnomes of the Cheese Forest
17 ~ Come to the Feast
18 ~ Thimble-Smith, Thorax & Thedd
19 ~ Solomon the Smackle-Bat
20 ~ The Wimzy
21 ~ The Cricket Watcher
22 ~ The Smoggle-Wogg
23 ~ Ka-Biggely Fickle
24 ~ King Monster
25 ~ The Black Knight
    of Kur-Kaxurr Castle
26 ~ The Spider Web
27 ~ Clarence the Cowardly Vampire
28 ~ The Little Man with the Red Teeth
29 ~ The Rhyme of
    Rebus the Surrealist Wizard
30 ~ O Where is the Woodpecker
31 ~ The Kyth-Dryl
32 ~ The Thing in Skegemog Lake
33 ~ The First Gryphon
34 ~ Out of My Mind
35 ~ The Goth Mime
36 ~ The Wise Ancient Tree
38 ~ The Parliament of Owls
40 ~ New Leaves
43 ~ The Great Epic Quest
    of Professor Stitch-Wicket
58 ~ Medusa's Dilemma
60 ~ The Paper Doll
61 ~ Night Frights

62 ~ The Witch in my Attic
63 ~ The Towel Monster
65 ~ The Book Beast
66 ~ Old Man Brownie
67 ~ The Kookaburra
68 ~ The Bottle Opener
69 ~ The Invisible Poem
70 ~ Book Worms
71 ~ The Peanut Vendor
72 ~ The Song
73 ~ One-Sided
74 ~ Monsters in my Head
76 ~ A Dog's Tale
77 ~ Success
78 ~ The Stories Inside Me
79 ~ A Butterfly in the Right Corner
80 ~ Remote Control
81 ~ Mom's Remedy
82 ~ Best School Ever
83 ~ Rock n' Roll Pizza Palace
90 ~ Recess
91 ~ Sidewalk Special
92 ~ The Troll Behind the Hedge
94 ~ Long Day
95 ~ Nothing Will Happen
96 ~ Stuck
97 ~ The Place Behind the Rain
99 ~ The Boy Who Looked Up
118 ~ One More Poem

Gnomes of the Cheese Forest
and Other Poems

GNOMES OF THE CHEESE FOREST
* with a nod to G.K. Chesterton

Listen in close, and I'll read you a rhyme
of a secret I've kept for a very long time,
for poets aplenty speak often of trees,
but silent are they — on the subject of cheese.*

Where does it come from, this cheesy delight?
You may have been told (by those knowing and bright)
that it's made in a dairy or old farmers' homes,
but in truth...

For hidden in forests all over the earth
are neighborly gnomes making music and mirth,
with lyrics in language from ages of old
(some form of Norwegian, or so I am told).

All in one chorus, a tiny gnome choir
erupts into song with each voice lifted higher,
and as the wood echoes with silvery sound,
up come the trees made of cheese from the ground.

With every aria, ballad, and hymn,
melted cheese drips from the tips of each limb,
and once their great trunks become fuller in size,
that's when the whip-poor-wills come from the skies...

What do the whip-poor-wills do, you may ask?
They come to perform a most delicate task.
Somehow or other, they pick the trees clean
(but this is a process that no one has seen).

The cheese is collected, and fully inspected
(a special procedure, refined and perfected).
The gnomes load it up into tiny clay jars,
which whip-poor-wills carry up into the stars.

The jars travel far under feathers in flight,
delivered to every cheese shop in sight.
The cheese is then packaged and sorted by weight,
and now you know how it ends up on your plate.

And that is my story...I hope that it pleases
to know the true origin of all your cheeses,
so next time you have some (on picnics in spring),
give thanks to the gnomes — and you may hear them sing.

COME TO THE FEAST

Calling all gremlins and goblins and ghouls,
   rag dolls and wretches and unholy fools,
banshees and boojums, each bogey and beast,
   come to the table — be part of our feast!

Come every witch with a twitch in their eye,
   punks and pickpockets who litter and lie,
Vermin and vampires, tricksters and tramps,
   wandering wights with no light in their lamps.

Bring in the bridge-keepers, fidgets and freaks,
   mutants and misanthropes, golems and geeks.
Welcome all creatures — there's plenty to eat!
   (And if *you'd* like to join us, we'll save you a seat.)

THIMBLE-SMITH, THORAX, and THEDD

The Great Bloody Battle of Goblin-Butt Hill
had left many missing or dead,
and no one remained to tell of its terrors
but Thimble-Smith, Thorax, and Thedd.

But Thorax was blinded, Thimble-Smith's mute,
and Thedd is in shock from the stress,
so what really happened that horrible day
is pretty much anyone's guess.

SOLOMON THE SMACKLE-BAT

Solomon the Smackle-Bat
sits alone in sorrow,
wondering if somebody
has some wings
that he could borrow.

THE WIMZY

The Wimzy is a gentle beast
who feeds on fish and squid,
and even though he likely could,
he'd *never* eat a kid.

He seems to be quite harmless.
I really wouldn't fret.
(Still, I'd never recommend
you keep one for a pet.)

THE CRICKET WATCHER

I hear there lives a creature
            who sits and watches crickets,
wherever he may find them,
            in parks or darkened thickets.
Day and night, he watches
            for hours back to back,
and when his belly grumbles,
            he has one for a snack.

THE SMOGGLE-WOGG

The Smoggle-Wogg stays in his cave,
and he will not come out.

He used to be daring and brave,
now he will not come out.

His cave is disheveled and dim,
but he will not come out.

I wonder what happened to him...
why will he not come out?

KA-BIGGELY FICKLE

Ka-Biggely Fickle sits in the trees,
gazing in wonder at all that she sees.
She takes it all in,
and then, with a grin,
she closes her eyes to catch a few Zs.

KING MONSTER

King Monster rules with an IRON FIST!
(At least, he wishes he could.
The real problem is — he doesn't have hands.
He just has one really big foot.)

THE BLACK KNIGHT OF KUR-KAXURR CASTLE

The Black Knight of Kur-Kaxurr Castle,
who leaves horrible plague and pestilence
behind in his wake...

whose imperious presence makes
even the most lionhearted knights
tremble in a stinging, cold sweat...

whose burning breath scalds the air
and searing rage scours his victims
with an appalling absence of mercy...

whose very name should never
be uttered by meek mortal men,
lest panic run rampant in the streets...

surveys the land
and plots its destruction
as he sits upon
his ostrich.

THE SPIDER WEB

A spider had finished her web one day,
when along came a fly on his way to the bay.

The fly was astounded! He paused in his flight,
and onto a branch he came down to alight.
The web had entranced him — he never had seen
a thing of such beauty, so fine and pristine.

He said to the spider, *What wonder is THIS?*
My many eyes burst at this visual bliss!
What you have done is a true work of art,
an honest expression that comes from your heart!

The way you have crafted each strand with such care,
and stitched them together to hang in the air,
the skill and precision, the perfect machining,
it's all the while subtle and layered with meaning!

My mind cannot fathom the sense of release
that touches my soul through this masterpiece!
What hath inspired this glorious feat?

The spider said,
    I made it so I can eat.

CLARENCE
THE COWARDLY VAMPIRE

Clarence the Cowardly Vampire
  has a life that is very complex.
Blood is his favorite beverage,
  but he's ever so fearful of necks.

THE LITTLE MAN WITH THE RED TEETH

I remember the first time I saw him,
while walking along by the heath.
At the end of the street,
still on his feet,
was the little man with the red teeth.

Leaves in the wind swirled around him,
as he stood there — silent as stone.
His stature was small,
not moving at all,
and his grin chilled me down to the bone.

My very nerves trembled in warning,
but naught could I whimper or shout.
Why his teeth are that way,
I really can't say,
and I surely don't wish to find out.

For years I have seen him in places,
in corners above and beneath.
It's not what I wanted,
but still I am haunted
by the little man with the red teeth.

THE RHYME OF
REBUS THE SURREALIST WIZARD

Elephant and cabbage, suitcase in the soup,
pile of rotting lobsters in a melting chicken coop.

Salamander sandwich, mustache on a cat,
dancing alligator with a poodle for a hat.

Fuzzy watermelon, Amish chandelier,
hippo on piano with a pickle in its ear.

Floating purple camel, squishy kangaroo,
wombat waffles, turtle cake, and helicopter stew.

Fish!

O Where is the Woodpecker

O where is the woodpecker with the white bill,
and where is his short trumpet call?

>Did he fly to wherever the unicorns went?
>Has anyone seen him at all?

>>Did he spirit away to that in-between space
>>where unfinished dreams go to chill?

>>>Is that question you find
>>>in the nook of your mind
>>>with the woodpecker and his white bill?

THE KYTH-DRYL

On fringes of the forest
where the chuck-will's-widow calls,
the village is bewitched by
that which lurks outside its walls.

For when the mist is rising,
and the darkest night is deep,
around each sleepy living soul
the vampyr dragons creep.

The locals call them *Kyth-Dryl*
from the elders' native tongue.
Their presence is a warning
for the old ones and the young.

For they only drain the blood
of those who've given up on life,
who don't see any hope
beyond their struggle and their strife.

So though there may be seasons
when you're sad or most in need,
do not remain there long enough
to let the Kyth-Dryl feed.

THE THING IN SKEGEMOG LAKE

You may have heard tell of monsters that dwell
under waters, though many be fiction or fake,
but every good sleuth knows the terrible truth
of the ominous Thing down in Skegemog Lake.

None have experienced its beastly appearance
(at least, that is, none who are well and alive).
The only such race that has gazed at its face
are the loons, as they go deep beneath for a dive.

They slip down below, and only they know
how to talk to this Thing that no mortal can find.
In darkness of night, when the lake has no light,
the loons come up singing what's on the Thing's mind.

When memories it shares are filled with despair,
the loons fill the air with their long lonesome wails,
but if they come after with trembling laughter,
the Thing may be telling more whimsical tales.

There's many a story of ghosts in their glory,
and mariners' ballads that make your heart ache,
but no lochs or lagoons share the secrets of loons
who speak with that Thing down in Skegemog Lake.

THE FIRST GRYPHON

My father was a lion.
My mother was an eagle.
They were sent away to prison,
for their marriage wasn't legal.

So here I am, not much to do,
except to live my life.
I hope some others break the law,
so I can find a wife.

OUT OF MY MIND

I took a look inside my mind,
and found it full of clutter.
Threads of thoughts, all scattered about,
colliding into one another.

I found it a strange, mysterious place
with the mark of a brilliant Inventor,
but here I had gone and dirtied it up,
putting myself in the center.

For all of my thoughts were smaller than I,
and I was the one who controlled them,
but they wouldn't listen — they got so confused,
no matter how much I told them.

So I took a look *outside* my mind,
and much to my shock and surprise,
I felt very small from the size of it all
and at first I averted my eyes.

As the fog lifted, my perspective shifted.
I didn't feel quite so confined,
so as a good way to spend more of the day,
I'd rather be out of my mind.

THE GOTH MIME

The Goth Mime thinks of somber songs,
and all things dark and grey,
but just how dark we'll never know,
because he doesn't say.

THE WISE ANCIENT TREE

Deep in the woods lives a wise ancient tree.
I knew he was someone I simply must see,
for he's been alive since the dawning of time.
He must know each lesson — he must know each rhyme.

He may know the reason our world is so dark,
and harbor great secrets submerged in his bark.
He might have the answers to life's many mysteries.
The tales he could tell — the legends, the histories!

I went to the forest and found him, quite silent.
He looked calm and peaceful, and not at all violent.
I pleaded, *O Tree, I have so much to ask.*
What is life's purpose? What's our true task?

I've come for the answer, the key to it all.
How shall we live? Will we prosper or fall?
He took a deep breath,
    fixed eyes on me,
        and said,
            Beats me, Sucker. I'm only a tree.

THE PARLIAMENT OF OWLS

The Parliament of Owls will now come to order.
Something must be done about this trouble at the border.

Now I'm not one to meddle in the business of ferrets
or disturb the operations of the Company of Parrots,
but as the noted chairman of this most distinguished board,
I have to say, the murder of crows should never be ignored!

The local Mob of Kangaroos is getting out of hand,
and the Gang of Turkeys has another siege of herons planned.
If what they teach in Schools of Fish does not change for the better,
I think we should address to them a reprimanding letter.

If this madness doesn't stop, our Regiment of Flamingoes
may need to be enlisted to dispel that Pack of Dingoes.
It's disgraceful from my point of view, and I would like to stress
the sloth of bears and pride of lions put us in this mess.

But now it's getting late my friends, the dawn is drawing near,
so the Congress of Baboons will have to take it all from here.

NEW LEAVES

The fairies work hard
in each garden and yard,
flitting through crystals
    and patches of clover.
They're found every spring
flying 'round on the wing,
looking for new leaves
    and turning them over.

THE GREAT EPIC QUEST
OF PROFESSOR STITCH-WICKET

Long, long ago in a time now forgotten,
when oceans had not yet turned blue,
there lived a professor who left on a quest
from his home where the wild woods grew...

His name was Professor Tobias Stitch-Wicket,
and all the wood knew he was wise.
He knew every creature, right down to each feature
of habitat, species and size.

    He knew every bird, each badger and beaver,
    and every opossum and otter.
    He knew every bug on the whole forest rug,
    and all things that swam underwater.

        By day he would talk over tea with the waxwings,
        to learn about berries and fruits.
        By night he would hang with the owls who sang,
        and learned all their various hoots.

            The wolves would entrust him with many dark secrets,
            the bears would discuss many issues,
            and listening close to their stories morose,
            the Professor used fig leaves for tissues.

                He was there when each duckling emerged from its egg,
                he welcomed each fawn that was born,
                and for every beast who was told *Rest in Peace*,
                with all of the wood he would mourn.

And so it was, one day he happened to notice,
while wandering along through the trees,
the moles in the ground were not to be found,
and neither their scent in the breeze.

    The woodpecker with the white bill had just vanished,
    and so had the great spotted shrew.
    The giant brown bear was no longer there,
    the weasel and wolverine too.

        The white-speckled deer, the cackling goose,
        the rabbit with stripes on its face,
        the kangaroo rat and the little black bat
        were gone without remnant or trace.

He went around asking if others had seen 'em,
but nobody knew where they were.
The Wise Ancient Tree, as an interviewee,
could not answer, consult or confer.

He questioned the loons down at Skegemog Lake,
but no solid answers they gave.
He tried dialogue with the old Smoggle-Wogg,
but he wouldn't come out of his cave.

And so the Professor, like any good scholar,
consulted his beakers and books.
He measured and mused with tools that he used
on evidence hidden in nooks.

With samples from bushes and burrows and bark,
he weighed against paths of migration,
and lined up his jars with patterns of stars
in precise and intense calculation.

Despite all his desperate study and science,
his findings had all come up short.
For creatures so dear to just *disappear*,
the reason he could not report.

But one little clue had stood out in his mind,
for 'round the wood, rumors were spreading,
and breaches of trust were being discussed
by those who knew where things were heading.

They spoke of machines made of metal and murk,
hard at work on something called *cities*.
They grew very quickly, and spread very thickly,
according to plans by committees.

The deafening din of these cities that grew,
the dirt and the smoke they created,
the Professor coughed, *Have they scared the beasts off?*
Is that why their homes are vacated?

If this is what's happening, where have they gone?
*Surely they must be **some**place.*
The Earth is so wide with places to hide,
I'd think they are still on its face.

He stayed up all night chewing on his wood pipe,
and at breaking of dawn, made a vow:
Leave the forest behind, for his friends he must find,
and he had to get started right now.

He raided his workshop of treasures and trinkets,
collected each bottle and spoon,
took furniture, fabric, and pieces of drab brick
to build a big hot-air balloon.

After a fortnight of sawing and sewing,
the gigantic vessel was ready,
with plenty of fire to help it climb higher,
and bags of earth keeping it steady.

The forest folk gathered to bid their farewell
as Tobias Stitch-Wicket ascended,
balloon sailing high and touching the sky
on a day when the weather was splendid.

But not every moment was pleasant as this
as the journey continued each day,
for hurricanes, lightning, and dangers so frightening
were coming the Professor's way.

Though no one has seen him for many a season,
his legend now faded to fog,
some say his balloon is still tracing the moon,
and peers its way out of the smog.

    Looking through scopes and his gadgets of glass,
    he seeks after inklings and clues,
    for any true sign of companions so fine,
    and any encouraging news.

        So keep your eyes open for hints of his shadow
        in places where forests have stood,
        and help the Professor along in his quest
        to find the lost beasts of the wood.

MEDUSA'S DILEMMA

Medusa has bad luck with barbers
(just from the snake bites alone).
When she goes to pay
at the end of her stay,
the cashiers keep turning to stone.

THE PAPER DOLL

I once had a nice paper doll.
   She was pretty and precious and small.
But one day at play,
   the wind blew her away,
and now I can't find her at all.

   Did she drift off to Montreal?
Or maybe as far as Nepal?
   I hope and I pray
that she is OK.
   Maybe one day she will call.

NIGHT FRIGHTS

I'm afraid to sleep tonight,
for when I close my eyes,
the boogeymen I saw last time
could catch me by surprise.

    I dreamt about this guy
    who makes a funny face,
    by sticking out his tongue
    from behind his hiding place.

        He has a little lion
        who has a wicked laugh.
        His eyes are big as dinner plates,
        his tongue is torn in half.

            I don't know where they come from,
            or why they're in my head.
            I really hope they go away,
            so I can go to bed.

THE WITCH IN MY ATTIC

I went up to my attic,
the walls were black as pitch,
and in my flashlight's halo I am sure I saw a witch.
   She sat there in the corner,
   hunched up in her cloak,
   stared at me with eyes of glass and reached out with a croak.
Down the stairs I stumbled,
and tried to catch my breath.
One look at her crooked face had frightened me to death.
   That night, from the attic,
   a crunching sound I heard,
   as if someone was chewing on the dry bones of a bird,
and in-between the crunches,
I heard a dreadful whine,
as if a cat was mewing through a muzzle made of twine.
   So that is why I always sleep to
     sounds of radio static,
       to drown out all the noises
         from the witch up in my attic.

THE TOWEL MONSTER

The Towel Monster waits for you to come out of the bath.
He likes to FEAST on little kids who tread across his path.

When your toes caress the floor, all dripping, soaking wet,
he takes his chance — he POUNCES and he snares you like a net!

He chews you up and swallows you in two blinks of an eye,
and then the Towel Monster BURPS and spits you out — all dry.

Clarence the Cowardly Vampire from Page 27
has kindly volunteered to demonstrate how to read the poem
on the opposite page.

Simply turn the book around and hold it in front of a mirror.

(It is most effective if read in the dark, by the light of a single candle or flashlight.)

THE BOOK BEAST

When you opened this book,
you awakened a beast
who lives in the depths of its ink.
It could now be anywhere,
under your bed,
or growing its skin in your sink.
Its fingers are slimy,
its teeth are like nails,
and the worst part (I hate to remind you)
is if you should happen to
put this book down,
it'll swallow you whole from behind you.

OLD MAN BROWNIE

Old Man Brownie
 lives behind the wall.
  I've seen him in the bedroom,
   the kitchen,
    and the hall.
     He's slippery and sneaky,
      and silent as a mouse.
       I think he is the reason
        things go missing in our house.

THE KOOKABURRA

Mommy, there's a kookaburra knocking at our door.
He's in a suit and tie — he must have bought them from a store.
I think he wants to sell something, but what I cannot say.
Should we let him come inside, or make him go away?

THE BOTTLE OPENER

I often think of the bottle opener
sitting inside my drawer.

I wonder if she looks at her life,
and longs for something more.

Perchance she deeply desires to dance
as a principal in the ballet,

and pirouette 'cross the kitchenette
'stead of opening bottles all day.

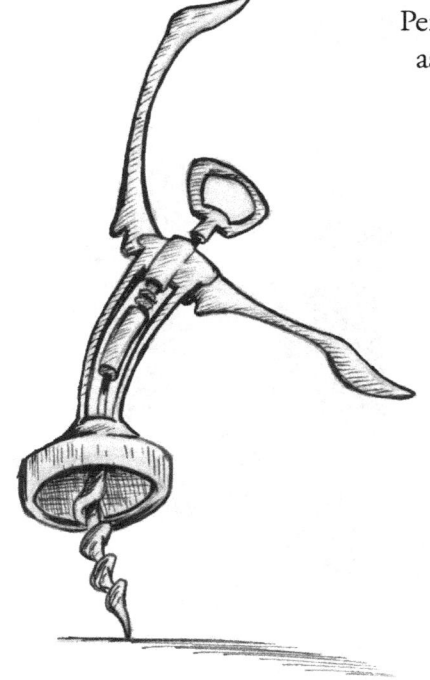

THE INVISIBLE POEM

BOOK WORMS

The pages stick together,
the bindings are all frayed.
There's pools of slime where
all the new releases are displayed.
The walls are wet and smelly,
the shelves are full of germs.
Things haven't been the same
since our library got worms.

THE PEANUT VENDOR

There's a monkey selling peanuts
at the corner of my street,
but I sense that he is someone
it'd be better not to meet.

THE SONG

In a dream, I heard the song
that makes the planets spin,
the song that played when all was made,
the first there's ever been.

I knew it once it graced my ear,
every note and verse.
I knew each part and word by heart,
with no need to rehearse.

I sang along with all my heart,
until my throat was sore,
'til I awoke when morning broke,
remembering it no more.

ONE-SIDED

They told me that this thing

       would be lots of fun to ride

             but I must have missed the part

                   about someone on each side.

MONSTERS IN MY HEAD

All day long I was attacked
by monsters in my head.
The **Doo-It-Laytr** came to roost,
with his best friend **Inn-Stedd**.

        The **Noh-Good** and the **Wai-Bothyr**,
        the **Yerr-Nott-Goodie-Nuff**,
        the **Yoo-Sukk** and **Yerr-Werthliss**,
        the **Doomorr-Yoosless-Tuff**,

                the **Ai-Quitt** and the **Ai-Givvup**,
                the **Hyde-It** and the **Hiddit**
                were all obliterated by
                the **Doo-It-Now** and **Diddit**.

A DOG'S TALE

I've chased this thing for ages,
but now I've come to see
the object I've been chasing
was always part of me.

SUCCESS

They say unless you make enough,
your life won't count for squat.
They say you're nothing
if you don't have limos or a yacht.

Unless you have good grades, they say,
and lots of education,
you'll never get a chance
to have a valid occupation.

You'd best invest in stocks and bonds,
or you'll be left behind.
You need to buy a fancy suit
and join the daily grind.

They say success is only made
through fame or a degree,
but I slayed the Beast of Skuffle-Tor
when I was only three.

THE STORIES INSIDE ME

There are stories inside me.
They want to get out.

They **groan** and they **grumble**,
      they SCREAM and they SHOUT.
They claw at my heart,
    tear at my brain,
      shiver and quiver and drive me insane.

They quiet down sometimes,
but then,
before long…

they stir from their slumber…and join in the throng
of pounding the pavement and shaking the gate,
desperate to try and
escape their estate,
saying…

PLEASE let us go! Do not keep us hidden!
We promise that we will behave if we're bidden!
Give us our freedom and silence our rage
from not being able to dance on the page!
If you keep us here, we fear we will DIE!
Save us, PLEASE SAVE US!!! the stories they cry,

Shall we wither away,
    or rot 'til we stink,
      because of those awful words…

        "what will they think?"

A Butterfly in the Right Corner

I'd like to draw for each person I see
a picture of me,
my house and a tree,
and a butterfly in the right corner,
so if they are sad,
or lonely, or mad,
or if they are missing their mom or their dad,
they'd smile if they knew that they constantly had
a butterfly in the right corner.

REMOTE CONTROL

I wish you had a remote control,
so I could watch you
frame
by
frame,

to turn YOU UP,
TUrn you down, or
mute you — when I want to.

To fast-forward you when I'm impatient,
STOP you when I've had enough,

but mostly — to pause you.

So you would never grow up.

            Or rewind you
        again,
    and again,
and again,

but my favorite button
would be

▶ PLAY

MOM'S REMEDY

I had a sore throat,
so Mom gave me some honey
in a spoon
and I thought that it tasted real funny,
so I shouted,
AAAGGHHH!!!!!!!
It's like JELLY!!!!
It's ICKY!!!
It's GROSS
and ALL SLIMY
and SILKY
and STICKY!!!

I don't like it!
I - pppffffffttttttt!!!
I don't want —

Hey, it worked!

BEST SCHOOL EVER

M<small>OMMY</small>!!! **Guess what?!?**

The teacher said — we're getting
    our own UNICORNS in school!!!!!
        She said we'll have matching outfits,
                it's gonna be so cool!!!

    We also have a field trip to the wildlife sanctuary!
        It's on the island,
           so guess what else?!?

          We get to ride a FAIRY!!!

Rock n' Roll Pizza Palace

If you want some fun on your birthday,
a music-and-laughter-filled mirthday,
there's no place from Denver to Dallas
like the ol' Rock n' Roll Pizza Palace!

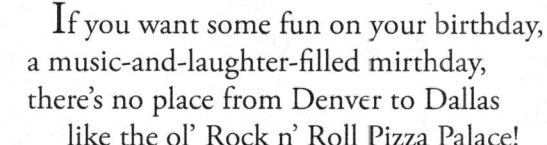

Your friends are delighted to meet you,
 a friendly bear strolls out to greet you,
with singin' and dancin' and jokin',
 and video games for a token.

Amidst all the lights and the noise,
 they got a full gift shop of toys.
The pizza is loaded on top,
 and refills are endless on pop.

Then slowly…the lights will go out,
you all give a sugar-fueled SHOUT,
and run to the stage room location,
to watch in great anticipation.

The red curtains open (real slow),
and then it is time for the show!
You're ready — with pizza in hand,
to ROCK with the world's greatest band…

On the left stage is **Johnny T. Hogg**,
    the Honky-Tonk Country Star Dog.
He twangs his guitar with a howl,
    playing cowboy songs with his pet owl.

On the right stage is **Count FrankenMorgan,**
    a bat with a haunted pipe organ.
He plays spooky songs of all types,
    as spider webs stir on his pipes.

And then — on the big center stage,
playing classics from rock's Golden Age,
Flash Mingo and **Monkey Man Zippo**,
with band leader **Doctor Hip Hippo**.

The room starts to rumble and shake,
    as you blow out the flames on your cake.
The lights flood the stage (right on cue),
    as they sing *HAPPY BIRTHDAY TO YOU!*

We'll dance and we'll party 'til late
on the day you turn seven or eight,
for there's no place from Denmark to Dallas
like the ol' Rock n' Roll Pizza Palace.

RECESS

The playscape is the mother ship,
this piece of wood — my blaster.
The tunnels are escape pods.
The yellow one goes faster.

The gravel is hot lava
spread under the slide.
The jungle gym's the cell bay
with the princess trapped inside.

The swingset is the hangar
for the rebels' fighting ships.
The space battle commences
as we improvise our scripts.

We've been to every planet
and defeated every foe
in our galaxy so far away
and so, so long ago…

SIDEWALK SPECIAL

Come and get your beetles, your weevils and your worms.
Don't forget your fungus, and your mud pies full of germs.

Buy a batch o' rotten fruit I found under the fence,
and I'll throw in some centipedes for only fifty cents.

We got a deal on roadkill — the finest stuff in town.
It comes in every color, from darkish-grey to brown.

You'll never find a better price for maggots, slugs or snails,
so I have no idea why I can't make any sales.

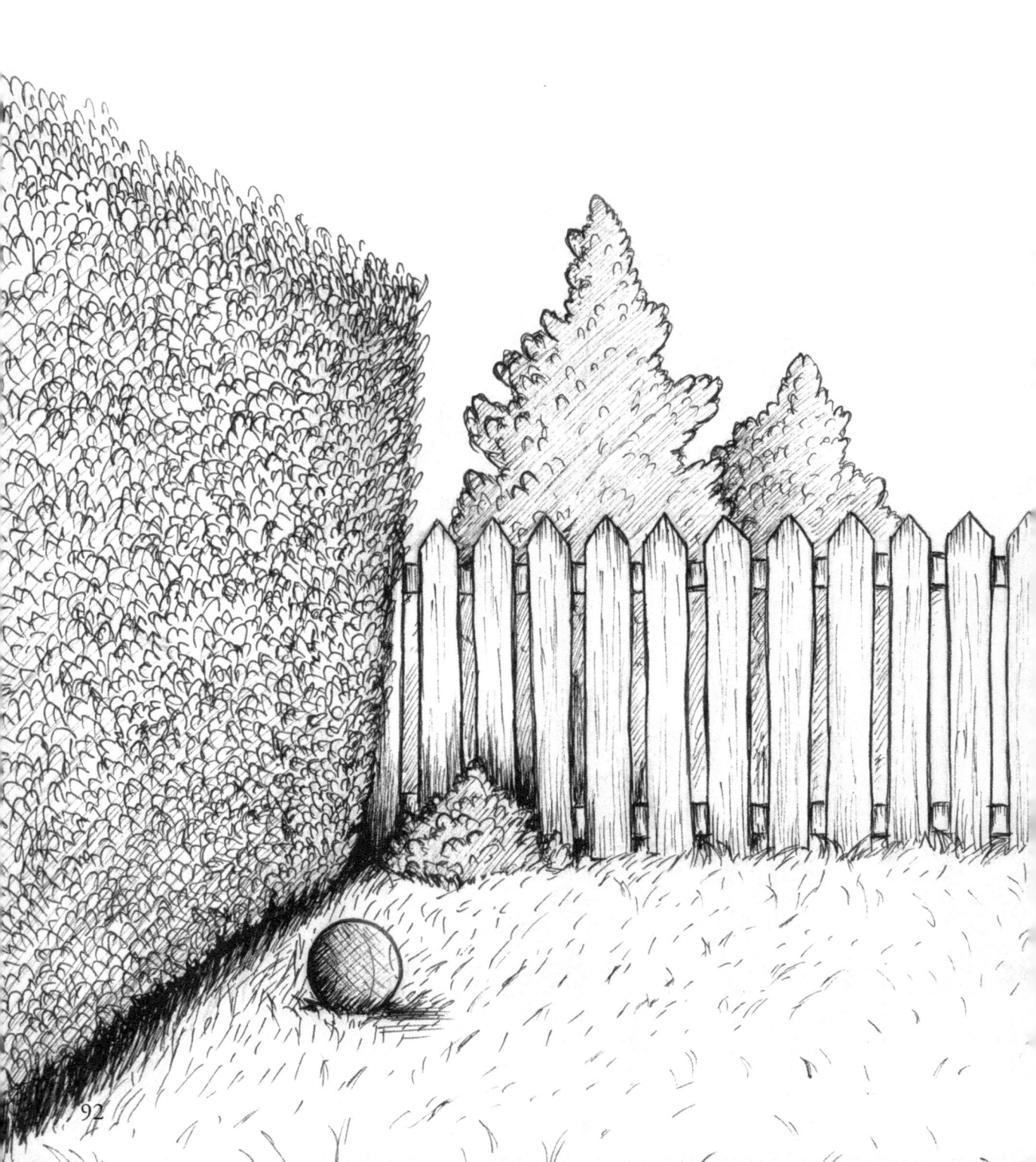

THE TROLL BEHIND THE HEDGE

The end of my backyard is bordered by a hedge,
and every now and then at play, my ball rolls to its edge.

It's troubling when this happens, for where the yards divide,
a troll lives there, behind the hedge, his favorite place to hide.

No one knows how many kids have gone to fetch their ball,
and disappeared without a trace — sneakers, hats and all.

That new kid Tommy came to play. We ran around the lawn.
I went inside to get a drink — when I came back, he was gone.

I didn't hear him struggle. I didn't hear him yell.
It must have broke his parents' heart. They moved away as well.

I wish I could do something, because it's very hard
to make new friends and keep them with a troll in your backyard.

LONG DAY

I
 was
  so
   tired.

    I had a long day.

     The kids had been washed
          and all put away.

      The dishes were changed
          and tucked into bed.

          I finally lay down to
                    rest
                     my
                      head...

                       and woke up
                        next morning
                         in the bathtub.

NOTHING WILL HAPPEN

I found a way to live worry free.
Nothing will happen if we stay by this tree.

We have all we need, just you and me.
Our families will come see us wed by the tree.

The children will play and giggle with glee,
dancing in circles right under our tree.

We'll never get bored, our children won't flee.
We'll grow old together, just us and our tree.

Why can't you see how happy we'll be
if you would just stay with me under the tree?

Why must you go? What is there to see?
What more could there be but this beautiful tree?

I wish you would stay — but just leave me be.
Nothing will happen here under my tree.

STUCK

I'm stuck in this stuff
and I cannot get out.
It's getting real tough
and I'm starting to doubt
if there's anyone there
who can get me un-stuck.
O please hear my prayer.
Get me out of this muck.

THE PLACE BEHIND THE RAIN

The place behind the rain
is where the tired people go,
 on the flipside of the falling sheets,
            the sleet and winter snow.

The people who are living there
have given up the fight
 to try and shut the darkness out
            by turning on the light.

On balconies they sit in rows
and watch the silent sea,
 thinking of the others who
            ignored their every plea.

They watch and wait for night to fall,
for stars they haven't seen,
 and wonder why they tried so hard
            to be a king or queen.

Remember what they told you,
Remember what they know,
 in the place behind the rain
            where the tired people go.

THE BOY WHO LOOKED UP

Have you heard the tale of Sebastian J. Thrupp, the boy who spent all of his time looking up?

With neck cradled back
and his chin pointed high,
he loved nothing more than to gaze at the sky.

He looked up at clouds as they slowly changed shape,
and saw each new butterfly make their escape.
He watched every bird, each airplane and jet,
and when it was raining, his face would get wet.

He'd sit there for hours just looking at trees,
and watching their long branches sway in the breeze.
He looked at the moon, followed Venus and Mars,
and never missed nights full of bright shooting stars.

But then as Sebastian looked up one fine day,
it happened that somehow his head *stuck that way*.
His mother freaked out — his father was shocked,
there was no question, his neck had just *locked!*

The doctor tried all of his needles and drills,
muscle relaxants and solvents and pills,
but with all that he tried and all that he did,
there was nothing that managed to help the poor kid.

But Sebastian, he didn't seem worried one bit.
He simply found ways to adapt and submit.
He drank from a straw, and when it came to eating,
he lay on his stomach, like he did for reading.

His writing and homework were done the same way.
They let him lie down in his classroom each day,
and anytime he had to move looking forw'rd,
he rolled down the hall on his trusty skateboard.

But all other times when he didn't need
to be horizontal to eat or to read,
Sebastian was perfectly glad and content
to keep looking up with his neck sharply bent.

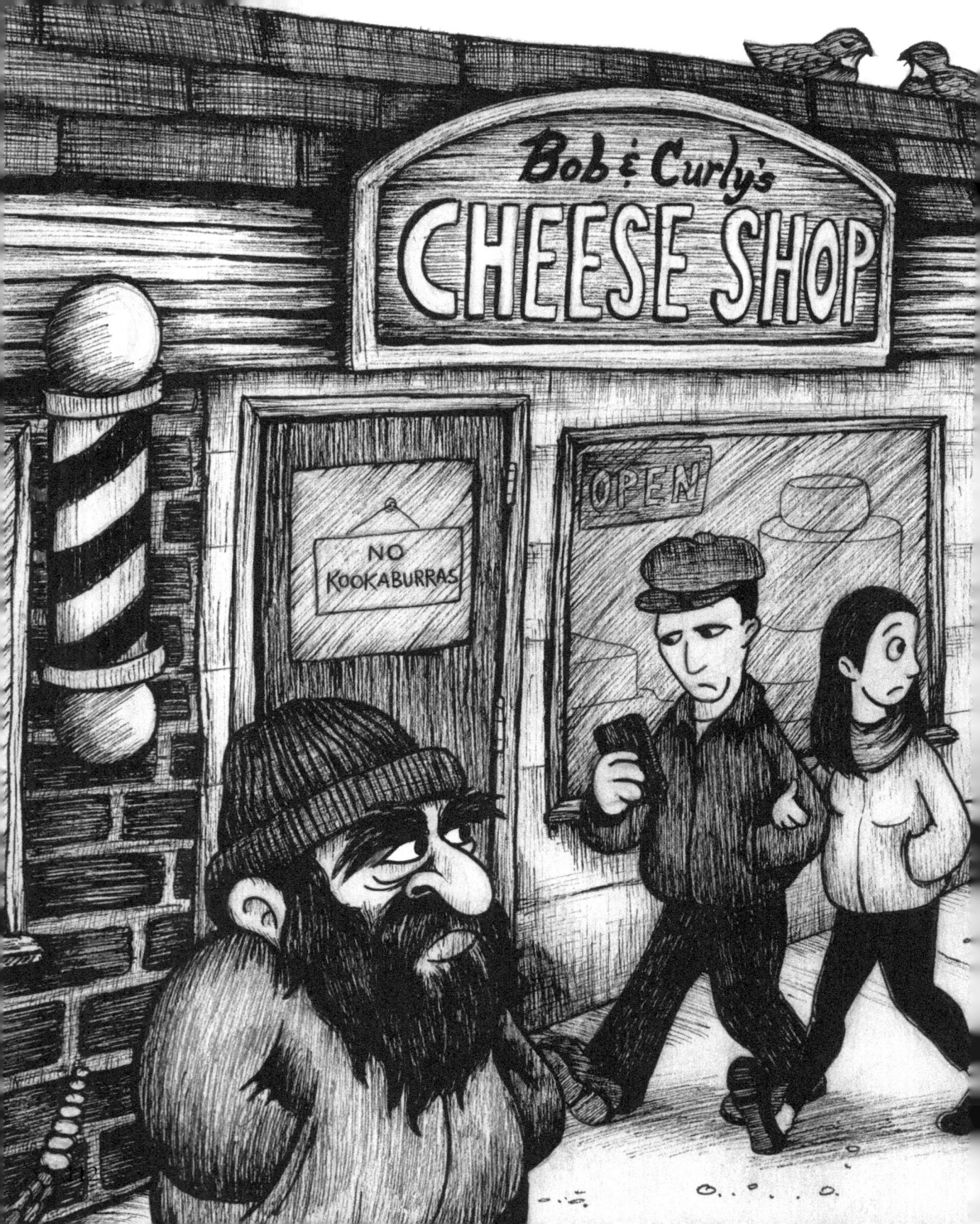

And so curiosity spread through the town
by others who always looked forward or down.
They said, *What's he looking at? What does he see?
Why is this boy looking up constantly?*

So some of the people, they gave it a try,
and spent more time staring up into the sky.
It was boring at first, and their necks became sore,
but after awhile they were doing it more.

As they looked upwards, they marveled in wonder
at all of the things they were living lives under.
Each night and day they could see something new,
so they told their friends, and they did it too.

All through the town, their necks locked in place,
with heads stuck forevermore pointed to space,
And O! What they saw, as they kept looking up...

...all because of a boy named Sebastian J. Thrupp.

ONE MORE POEM

I sat down to write one more poem,
but nothing has come to my head.
Maybe I need to go for a walk,
or maybe I'll just go to bed.

But hey, you're still here…
would you like to write one instead?

ABOUT THE AUTHOR & ILLUSTRATOR

Ken Priebe likes to write books, draw pictures, make movies, and bring puppets to life. Born and raised in Grosse Pointe, Michigan, he has worked and taught for many years in the world of animation and lives near Vancouver, Canada with his wife, two children, two cats, one dog, and the monsters in his head. He likes birds, too.

Visit gnomesofthecheeseforest.blogspot.com for
a look behind-the-scenes of this book and
where to find updates on other projects.

CPSIA information can be obtained
at www.ICGtesting.com
Printed in the USA
LVHW100341180820
663483LV00002B/543